The
Clubhouse
Mystery

PHOTO: JOE BUTLER

ERIKA MCGANN lives in Dublin in her own secret clubhouse (which is actually an apartment) and spends her time solving mysteries and having brilliant adventures (well, she writes about them anyway). She likes cold weather (because it's an excuse to drink hot chocolate by the gallon) and cheesy jokes (because cheesy jokes are always funny, even when they're not funny).

CASS and
THE BUBBLE STREET GANG

The Clubhouse Mystery

Erika McGann

illustrated by Vince Reid

THE O'BRIEN PRESS
DUBLIN

First published 2017 by
The O'Brien Press Ltd,
12 Terenure Road East, Rathgar,
Dublin 6, D06 HD27 Ireland.
Tel: +353 1 4923333; Fax: +353 1 4922777
E-mail: books@obrien.ie.
Website: www.obrien.ie

ISBN: 978-1-84717-920-3

1 3 5 7 8 6 4 2
17 19 21 20 18

Cover and internal illustrations by Vince Reid.
Printed and bound by Norhaven Paperback A/S, Denmark.

The paper in this book is produced using pulp from managed forests.

For Amara and Calla

Acknowledgements

As always, I'd like to thank my family; my mum, in particular, for the wonderful holiday in the beautiful house where I wrote this book. A big thanks to Vince Reid for the brilliant and funny illustrations that suit the story so perfectly. And a giant thanks to my editor, Helen Carr – I'm so glad I'm getting to work with you on this series.

Chapter One

Do you want to know a secret? Well, I can't tell you. I absolutely cannot tell you. It's the biggest, most exciting secret I've had in weeks, maybe even months. I mean, I could tell you, but then I'd have to kill you. So, you see, I absolutely cannot tell you …

All right, how about I tell you and you promise not to tell anybody else? Not even your best friend. Not even your pet. Not even your pet even if your pet is also your best friend. Cross your heart and hope to die? Okay then, you've twisted my arm.

We've built a fort. A secret fort. A *clubhouse*.

I probably should have mentioned first that I'm in a secret club. Well, here goes, the entire secret: I'm in a secret club and now we've got a secret clubhouse.

The idea came (as so many of my ideas do) from the desperate need to get out of the house and away from the annoying baby twins. It was Saturday morning and I had built an epic fort in the sitting room. It involved one sofa, one mop, two armchairs, two dining chairs, the pouffy/footstool thing that my mum likes, and five (that's right, FIVE) blankets. It was nearly tall enough to stand up in, there was a window (made using a bunch of clothes pegs off the washing line) through which I could watch TV, and the whole thing was protected by an invisible force field.

Unfortunately, although the force field was effective in keeping out aliens, monsters and Bigfoot, it was apparently no match for the annoying baby twins. They demolished the entire fort in about ten seconds flat.

'Daaad!' I yelled up the stairs. 'The twins wrecked my fort.'

'Did they?' he called back. 'Well, don't worry, honey, you can build it again.'

That didn't help at all.

'Muuum!' I yelled. 'The twins wrecked my fort.'

'They just want to play with you, Cass,' she called back. 'Why don't you pick something you can all play together?'

Play with the *annoying baby twins*? That's a ridiculous suggestion. Before they were born I might have thought it was a great idea. I'd had the house to myself for eight whole years – I was the queen of the castle, I ruled the roost – but when my parents told me I had two brothers or sisters on the way I was really excited. Two more kids, as funny and clever as me, to share adventures with and laugh at all my hilarious jokes? Bring it on.

But instead of two brilliant siblings my parents came home with Pippi and Ade; a pair of bulldozers in babygros. Pippi will chew anything she can get her grubby hands on. She puts EVERYTHING in her mouth. Ade, on the other hand, won't eat anything. Food goes in his hair or up his nose or on the floor or all over my dad's shirt. Come to think of it, I'm not sure I've ever seen any food go into Ade's mouth. Shouldn't he be hungry by now? Ugh, babies are weird.

I call them the annoying baby twins, but they aren't really babies anymore. They're two years old, which means they're even *more* annoying than they used to be. When they were babies, and couldn't walk yet, they could only chew and destroy anything in reach of their little arms. But now they're mobile. They're like two mini-Godzillas trampling everything in their path.

BREAKING NEWS:

This is Cass Okara reporting from downtown Tokyo, where residents are running for their lives from two hideous monsters that crawled out of the harbour this morning. Some of the city's most treasured buildings have already been destroyed, including the beloved Cass Towers – a brilliant structure designed and built by local genius Cass Okara. The whole city is in mourning. Back to you in the studio, Dave.

That was when I had the great idea of building a fort outside the house, where the twins couldn't wreck it. Then I had the *brilliant* idea that this new fort should be the clubhouse for our secret club. I always thought we needed one; what's a secret club without a secret clubhouse?

This is my best friend, Lex (which is short for Alex, which is short for Alexandria). She lives across the street from me. 'Where would we build it?' she asked when I told her my idea. 'In your back garden?'

'No way, the twins get into the back garden all the time. We need somewhere secret, so other people don't find it by accident.'

'Hmm, that's a toughie.'

We hmm'd for a bit, and then we hawed for a bit, and then Lex's granny poked her head around the door.

'I've got chocolate chip cookies and orange juice here for anyone who's hungry.'

Lex's granny lives two streets away, but she's in Lex's house a lot. She's awesome. When Lex's parents are out she lets us eat all the junk food we want, and she comes up with the best games when we're bored. One time it was *pouring* rain outside, and she dared us to go out into the back garden and make mud sculptures. Whoever made the biggest one got a lollipop. Lex made a dog standing up; it fell down so she made it into a dog lying down, but her mud was just too runny and in the end she called it a 'dog rug' because it was basically flat. Mine was the biggest and it *didn't* fall down (it was kind of a dolphin with legs). In making a flat dog and a leggy dolphin, all the mud from the flowerbeds ended up in the middle of the grass and Lex's parents were really mad. And when I got home and left mud trails through the hall my parents were really mad too. The mud sculptures were worth it though.

'I couldn't help overhearing' – Lex's granny put the tray on the floor and we grabbed some cookies – 'that you're looking for somewhere to build a fort.'

Note to self: Be quieter when talking about the secret clubhouse to secret club members.

'Maybe we are and maybe we aren't,' Lex said, trying to be mysterious.

Her granny smiled.

'Well,' she said, 'if someone did want to

build a secret fort, I happen to know of the perfect spot.'

'Where?'

'At the end of Mr McCall's field.'

Mr McCall's house is separate from the housing estate and it's giant. There's a big field behind it (that's after his big, massive garden, so it's miles away from the house) where he sometimes keeps a few horses, but there are none in there at the moment. I think he sold them all for loads of money.

'That's perfect!' I said.

'There's a hedge of tall trees down that end,' Lex's granny said, 'and plenty of bushes too, so the fort would be well hidden.'

I told you Lex's granny was great.

This is my other best friend, Nicholas

(which is long for Nick. I've tried calling him Nick lots of times, but he doesn't like it). He lives at the very end of our street, opposite the empty house. We're all a bit afraid of the empty house  because we're pretty sure it's haunted. Nicholas's dad says it's nonsense, and my mum says it's nonsense, which is why I think adults should never be allowed to investigate the paranormal. They've lost their sensitivity to ghosts and other weird stuff. Ever have your mum or dad tell you there's nothing under your bed when you absolutely *know* that there is? Yeah, me too. Dealing with ghosts and scary things should be left to the kids; we're the experts.

Anyway, we told Nicholas about the clubhouse plan and, as always, he had some concerns.

'What will we build it out of?' he asked.

'I dunno yet,' I said, 'but I'm going to scope out the area and maybe pick a tree for us to build it in. Then I'll know what stuff we need.'

'Where will we get the stuff we need?'

'I dunno yet, maybe from my shed at

home, or yours, or Lex's. There might be stuff in school we can use.'

'How will we keep it a secret if we need to ask for building materials?'

'I dunno yet,' I said, getting impatient. 'I'll figure it out.'

'But how—'

'That's enough questions.'

'I've got one more,' he said.

'No, that's your quota of questions for the day. You can't ask any more. If you want to ask any more you have to wait until tomorrow.'

'But how can we plan if I can't—'

'Urghh,' I growled, sticking my fingers in my ears, 'I'm not listening.'

He kept talking so I kept my fingers in my ears and went, 'la-la-la-la, la, la, la, la, laaaaaa,' until he rolled his eyes and stopped.

'Why don't we go take a look at the field now?' said Lex.

'Brilliant idea!' I said. 'We'll have to be in stealth mode though, because Mr McCall doesn't like children.'

'I heard he's got a mini-jail in his garden for kids who sneak onto his land. He keeps them there until the police arrive.'

'That's absolute rubbish,' I said, though I wasn't sure. 'Come on, let's go.'

'So,' Nicholas said as we left his room, 'if we need hammers and nails and things, where are we going to–'

'Urghh!' I closed my eyes and jammed my fingers in my ears again. Then I walked into the door on the way out and I didn't speak to Nicholas all the way to Mr McCall's field.

Chapter Two

So now you've met the three members of the Bubble Street Gang. That's the name of our club (don't say it out loud, it's a secret). It comes from the name of the street we all live on, except that that's actually *Berbel* Street (pronounced Burrrr-ble Street). Lots of people pronounce it wrong – as 'Bubble Street' – even the postman, but I can't really blame them. I used to say it wrong too. Until I was five, that is.

Still, we all decided that *Bubble* Street Gang sounds better than *Berbel* Street Gang (which sounds kind of lame), so that's what we are. The Bubble Street Gang. Anyway, back to the story.

We crept down the lane beside Mr McCall's field under cover of daylight (under cover of darkness would have been better, but it was four o'clock in the afternoon), and met our first obstacle. It was a cow. Or a bull, I'm not sure which. It was a large, light-brown, cow-like animal that stood between us and the hedge. It stared over the fence and chewed really slowly, like it was hatching an evil plan.

'I don't get it,' said Lex. 'Mr McCall's never had a cow before.'

'It's a bull,' said Nicholas. 'A cow would have udders.'

'Whatever it is,' I said, 'it's standing between us and our clubhouse. One of us will have to shoo it to the other end of the field.'

I waited for someone to volunteer. There

was silence for about five minutes.

'Oh, come on,' I said, 'it's not like it's a lion. You just have to say "shoo" and wave your hands and it'll move.'

'Off you go, then,' said Nicholas.

'Fine then, I will.'

To my friends I know I looked like a casual hero climbing over the fence with no regard for my own safety, but I was actually a little bit nervous. The bull kept blowing loudly out its nose which made my knees feel wobbly. I stayed a good distance away from it and said, 'Here, bull-y, bull-y, bull-y. Who's a good bull, huh?'

'It's not a dog,' said Nicholas, standing safely in the muddy lane. 'You have to treat it like a cowboy would.'

'What would a cowboy know about bulls?'

'That's their job, herding cows. They're *cow*boys.'

I rolled my eyes. 'Nicholas, you're so gullible, that's just a name. Cowboys ride *horses*.'

He rolled his eyes back at me and Lex jumped.

'Cass, look out!'

The bull had taken two steps in my direction. Then he stood still again and kept chewing.

'Actually,' I said, quickly climbing back over the fence, 'I think this bull might not shoo. He doesn't look very bright to me.'

'You mean he looks scary,' said Nicholas.

'No, he looks dim, and everybody knows dim cows don't shoo.'

'So we can't make our clubhouse here,' said Lex.

It seemed that way until I suddenly saw the value in a scary bull that doesn't shoo.

'Of course we can make it here, it's even more perfect!'

'How's that?' said Nicholas.

'The bull will scare off any intruders trying to get into our secret clubhouse. He'll be like a security guard.'

'Why would a secret clubhouse that nobody knows exists need a security guard?'

'Stop naysaying, Nicholas, no one likes a naysayer.'

'What's a naysayer?'

'A person who says nay a lot.'

'I didn't say nay, I don't even know what nay means.'

'It means no.'

'I didn't say no either.'

'I think a bull security guard sounds great,' said Lex, 'but how do *we* get to the secret clubhouse?'

'Easy,' I said. 'From the other side of the hedge.'

Nicholas gave me a disbelieving look but I pretended that it wasn't a big deal. And it really wasn't *that big* a deal.

The thing on the other side of the hedge that wasn't a big deal was a huge, wide, deep ditch with a stream running through it, that is impossible to cross.

'We can jump it,' I said.

'No,' said Nicholas.

'Run and jump. If we run really fast and then jump, right at the edge, we'll totally make it.'

'No.'

'I'll do it,' said Lex.

'No way,' said Nicholas, 'it's far too dangerous.'

I started lecturing Nicholas on his lack of commitment to the clubhouse, and he started lecturing me on safety in the workplace, and while we were arguing Lex jumped the stream. Totally jumped it. Like a giant frog. She ran really fast to the edge, jumped, grabbed hold of a saggy branch that was hanging over the ditch, and swung to the other side. She did land in a heap in a bramble bush, but apart from that it was a 10.0.

I don't think I've mentioned it yet, but Lex likes to climb things, and hang off things, and jump off other things. She's kind of like a monkey but without the tail. Lex can be pretty chatty with the gang, but she doesn't talk much in front of other people. She's shy and prefers to express herself through dangerous stunts. One time her parents made her sign up for the school play, hoping it would make her less shy, but Lex was a

no-show on the night. When her cue came she never appeared. Her parents didn't get to see her on stage, but if they had looked up they would have seen her dangling from the rafters.

After she'd crawled out of the bramble bush, Lex brushed herself off and said, 'Hang on a sec,' before diving back in. She reappeared dragging a plank of wood.

'Where did you get that?' I said.

'It was under the bushes. I think it's a broken bit off the fence.'

And, hey presto, we had a bridge to the secret clubhouse!

Now all we needed was an actual clubhouse, and I'd just seen the perfect spot – prepare to be green with envy. Here it is, the site of the soon-to-be clubhouse. It was too

The Clubhouse

Phase 1: Location confirmed

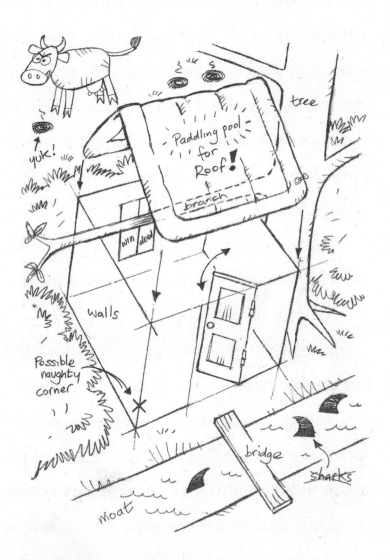

perfect to describe in words, so I had to draw a diagram.

I bet you're impressed. No? Really? You will be.

Imagine walls surrounding the space in the middle (maybe with a window if we can manage it), with an actual door that opens and closes, and a paddling pool (without water in it, obviously) hanging over the big branch as a waterproof roof. The paddling pool bit was my idea. Go on, call me a genius, you know you want to.

All right, so we had the perfect location for the clubhouse – complete with secret bridge entrance and giant snorting security guard – all we needed now were the materials to build it. This was going to take some thinking, and some borrowing and, if we get desperate, some stealing (is it still stealing if you're stealing from your own shed at home? I'm not sure, but I think probably not ... don't tell my parents though).

Chapter Three

'Who got a rabbit?'

'Nicholas. No, Lex. Lex got a rabbit.'

'Lex got a rabbit?'

My mum does this thing with her eyes when she suspects I'm lying about something. Her eyes go really wide and stay that way for as long as I'm talking, and if she still doesn't believe me when I'm finished her eyebrows go up as well. I was trying to get through this one little white lie without the eyebrows going up. White lies are a necessary evil for anyone with as many secrets as I have, and I'm very good at telling them. The secret to telling a believable lie is to add as much detail as humanly possible.

My mum's eyebrows hadn't gone up yet, but her eyes were definitely wide.

'That's funny,' she said, 'I met Lex's mum this morning and she never mentioned anything about getting a pet rabbit.'

'That's 'cos Lex didn't get a pet rabbit, it was actually her cousin. Her cousin, Ella. I forgot for a minute because Lex's granny brought the rabbit over to Lex's house for us to have a look at it, and then she was going to bring it back to Ella because it's Ella's rabbit. His name is Fleecy. Fleecy the rabbit. He's grey and white and really soft and sometimes he does this wiggly thing with his nose, like–'

'How come you're building a rabbit hutch for Lex's cousin Ella's rabbit, Fleecy?'

That was a good question. Why would I be

building a rabbit hutch for Lex's cousin Ella's rabbit, Fleecy? After a moment I said, 'Ella's really lazy.'

The eyebrows were twitching. 'Is that right?'

'Yeah, Lex was going on about how poor Fleecy would be stuck indoors all day because Ella would never get around to building him a hutch even though she said she would but she probably never would because she's really lazy and she never does anything she says she's going to do,' I said, watching my mum's forehead like a hawk. 'So then me and Nicholas said we'd help Lex build one. So that's why we need the stuff from the shed.'

At that moment the annoying baby twins actually did something useful. They had a big fight over a little yellow truck and my mum was distracted.

'Fine, fine,' she said, trying to separate the mini-monsters, 'but don't touch the toolbox in there. Only the stuff in the back, do you hear me?'

'Yes, mum. Thanks.'

Mission accomplished.

Inside the clubhouse it was kind of dark, but it was also brilliant.

'Our very own clubhouse,' said Lex, looking around.

'Where we can plan all our adventures, and *no one* can see or hear,' I said. 'But it's not finished yet. We need to decorate this place, and it needs a bit of furniture. A table we can draw our plans on, and some chairs.'

'And a floor,' Nicholas said, lifting up his

The Clubhouse

Phase 2: External structure complete

Ladies and gentleman, feast your eyes on the
architectural wonder that is the Bubble Street
Gang Clubhouse. With walls of solid chipboard,
joined with a mixture of wood glue and
play-dough, this Roman-style building boasts a
beautiful stream view and water-resistant roof.
Located in the much sought after area of Mr
McCall's hedge, this stunning field-side villa is
sure to be snapped up as soon as it hits
the market.
Bid early to avoid disappointment*.

*Bidding starts at €1,000,000

foot. His shoes were pretty mucky.

'Fine, a floor too,' I said, thinking, 'and I know exactly where we can get one of those.'

Our school is big into drama. It puts on more plays and musicals than all the other schools in town put together. That's mostly because of Ms Bulger. Ms Bulger used to be an actress; she was in two TV commercials and had three lines in a soap opera before she gave up a life of fame and fortune to follow her true vocation of becoming a teacher. Nicholas's dad once said she lives *vi-care-ee-ussly* through her students; I think that means she makes everyone do awful plays all the time so she can yell and pull out her hair.

The reason I mention Ms Bulger and all the drama is because, in the drama room, there's a roll of this dark-green foam that would be perfect for our clubhouse floor.

'No,' Nicholas said outside Ms Bulger's door, 'absolutely not. She'll think I'm joining the drama group.'

'Just say you want it for a special costume,' I said.

'What sort of costume would use green floor foam?'

'Why are you asking me? You're the expert.'

I should mention that Nicholas is a costume designer. He's always drawing disguises and costumes; not boring things like trousers and skirts, but interesting, useful things like a fireproof diving suit and anti-anti-gravity boots (they're boots that stick to the ground so you can't fly off into the sky. They don't sound that useful, but if the world got turned upside down you'd be sorry if you didn't have a pair).

I dragged Nicholas into the room before he could argue any more about the green foam. Ms Bulger was sitting at her desk, polishing a little golden Oscar statue. It's a replica. Ms Bulger never won an Oscar.

'Hello, Cass,' she said, then lit up when she saw who was behind me, 'and Nicholas! We don't see you in this room very often. Changed your mind about the Shakespearean musical medley next term?'

'Uh,' Nicholas stammered, 'no.'

I should also mention that Nicholas is an actor – not like one of the actors in one of Ms Bulger's plays, an actual actor – who has lessons with a serious acting coach and everything. The acting coach has a really long Russian name that I can't remember,

and he's really, really strict. Nobody else in school goes to serious acting lessons with a Russian teacher with a really long name, so Ms Bulger is always trying to get Nicholas to join the school drama group. He won't though, he says it's beneath him. His dad agrees.

'Well, if you were hoping to get into *The Sound of Music* this term,' Ms Bulger said, 'I'm afraid all the roles have been filled.'

'Oh, Nicholas was actually wondering if he could have some of that green foam stuff to make a costume,' I said.

'A costume for the play?' Ms Bulger asked.

She was looking at us with narrowed eyes, and I suddenly realised she might think we were setting up a rival drama company.

'Yes,' I said, 'for *your* play. He wants to help.'

'What costume in the play would use green foam?' the teacher asked.

'Grass,' I said, thinking on my feet.

'Grass?'

'Yes, grass. Isn't there grass on the mountains in *The Sound of Music*?'

Ms Bulger looked suspicious *and* confused now.

'Who would want to play grass?'

'Nicholas,' I said. 'He thinks it would be a gentle introduction into the drama group – your programme is very advanced, after all – and after he's played grass he may be ready for something more complicated.'

Ms Bulger looked confused for a few more moments, then burst into a great big grin.

'That's wonderful!' she said. 'Brilliant notion. Yes, yes, Nicholas, grass in *The Sound of Music* this term, and then we'll move you on to *Macbeth* and *Hamlet's* duet in the musical next term. Wonderful!'

'So we can take some of the green foam?' I said.

'Yes, absolutely, take the whole roll. You'll want to get your grass costume right, won't you Nicholas?'

I was beaming. A whole roll of the stuff would be plenty for the clubhouse floor (with enough left over for a grass costume too). I kept smiling politely at the teacher, trying to ignore Nicholas, who was staring at me like he was trying to explode my head with his mind.

Chapter Four

The green foam floor looked awesome. You could have stuck a net in the middle of the room and played tennis. But you can't plan wild adventures on a net, so we got a table instead; a fold-out one from Nicholas's aunt, who was chucking stuff out. She was also throwing out some old patio chairs so we got them too.

'I call the first official meeting of the Bubble Street Gang to order,' I said, banging an orange plastic hammer on the table. 'Cass – that's me – present. Lex?'

'Present,' said Lex.

'Nicholas?'

He sat in the corner and didn't answer. He was still mad at me over the whole grass in *The Sound of Music* thing, so I just banged the hammer again and said, 'All members present. First item on the agenda, emergency provisions for midnight feasts.'

Lex looked worried.

'Are we staying here overnight?' she asked.

'Maybe not,' I said, 'but if some catastrophe occurs while we're in here, like a zombie apocalypse or something, then we may need to stay here til dawn.'

'My mum will be really mad if I'm not home for dinner.'

'Well, there probably won't be a zombie apocalypse today so I'd say you're all right, but there could be one in the future so we need to make sure we have emergency provisions. Plus, it would be nice to have snacks for the meetings; cookies and things.'

'Gran's in my house today, so we could raid the cupboards in the kitchen. She'll let us take anything we want.'

'Perfect! And I've got half a chocolate gnome left that my cousin brought me from France. Nicholas?'

Nicholas just glared at me and I sighed.

'It's *one* play,' I said, 'and you don't even have to do anything, you just have to lie there.'

'It's a proper production with funding,' he snapped. 'That means it'll go on my acting resumé. My first acting job will always be *grass*.'

'Cheer up, everybody's gotta start somewhere. Did your dad make flapjacks this week?'

Nicholas threw open the door, which made the whole clubhouse shake, and marched out into the sunshine.

'I think that's a yes,' I said.

'Ooh, yum,' Lex said, clapping her hands, 'I love Nicholas's dad's flapjacks.'

'And some jelly beans, and some chocolate bourbons and, ooh, here take a bunch of these muffins with the gooey vanilla centre, I love those.'

Lex's granny had her head stuck in the treat cupboard in Lex's kitchen, throwing stuff behind her for us to catch.

'Your granny's the best,' I whispered to Lex, whose arms were filled with packets of crisps.

'I know,' she replied, catching another packet.

Nicholas was trying to squeeze two large bottles of fizzy orange into Lex's backpack when we heard a key turn in the front door.

'My mum!' Lex squealed.

'Battle stations,' her granny said. 'Hide the loot!'

We ran back and forth across the kitchen floor in a panic before Lex flung open the door of the washing machine and we all jammed the crisps and biscuits and fizzy orange inside, shutting the door just in time.

Lex's mum was talking as she walked into the kitchen.

'I bet she did,' she said before seeing all of us standing suspiciously in front of the washing machine. 'Speak of the devil!'

My mum walked in behind her.

'Speak of the devil indeed,' she said. 'I was just telling Karen about your fight with the twins the other day, honey, when they knocked down your fort in the sitting room. Remember? Kind of funny, wasn't it?'

'Hilarious,' I said, not smiling.

'The little angels,' Lex's granny crooned.

I'd never seen anyone look so casual. She leaned against the countertop with a cup of tea (that had appeared out of nowhere!) and smiled like a cuddly old granny from a cartoon. My mum and Lex's mum tilted their heads and beamed back; they think she's so sweet and innocent, but Lex's granny is some sort of diabolical genius. Some day I'm going to be just like her.

'How's the hutch coming along?' my

mum asked.

'The what?' said Lex's mum.

'The hutch. For Ella's new rabbit. What's it called again, Cass?'

'Eh, Fleecy,' I said.

My mum was looking right at Lex's granny. 'Didn't you bring him over to meet the girls at one point, Mrs Brooks?'

Lex's granny didn't even flinch.

'I did indeed,' she said. 'In fact, he's upstairs right now.'

'Oh, I'd love to see him. Cass says he's gorgeous.'

'No problem. You go get him, Lex, there's a good girl. Cass will help you.'

The two of us stood in front of the washing machine with no clue what to do. Lex's granny gave us a confident wink while our mums started quizzing Nicholas on his art stuff. Lex and I walked slowly from the room, slowly up the stairs, slowly into Lex's bedroom, then stood there totally perplexed.

'Why did you tell your mum Ella got a new rabbit?' Lex said.

'Because we needed the chipboard and stuff from the shed, so I told her it was for building a hutch.'

'Where are we going to get a rabbit?'

'Beats me. Your granny's landed us right in it.'

'Yeah, she does that sometimes. She says I need to learn how to improvise.'

Maybe Lex's granny had a point.

'Well then,' I said, suddenly confident, 'we need something that can pass for a fluffy grey and white rabbit.'

We chose a stuffed toy of Lex's that was the right colour. It was a weird sort of animal though – a wombat, or something – not a rabbit, so we wrapped it in a woolly blanket, like a baby, with just its nose peeking out.

'This would work fine from a distance,' Lex said, cradling the wombat-baby in her arms, 'but up close, no way.'

'Then we can't let them see it up close,' I said. 'Hmm, it's a shame we can't get into the back garden without going through the kitchen.'

'The back garden? Easy.' Lex opened her bedroom window and pointed to the drain-pipe on the wall. 'Shimmy down that, hop onto the roof of the shed, then just hang off the gable and drop to the grass. I do it all the time.'

I took one look at the long drop and decided my skills were needed elsewhere.

'You head down to the back garden,' I said. 'Take the rabbit with you so you can show him off from outside the kitchen, but keep your distance.'

I was about to ask if Lex could safely climb down while carrying the stuffed toy, but she'd already dropped him out the open window.

'What are you going to do?' she asked.

'I'm going back to the kitchen to make sure they don't look too close.'

Nicholas was giving the three women an in-depth description of his latest acting lesson. That was perfect; they were totally distracted. I tiptoed into the kitchen practically unseen (Lex's granny's gaze flickered for a moment, though she didn't give me away). Quiet as a mouse I crept to the back door, turned the key and popped it into my pocket.

'Fleecy wasn't upstairs at all,' I said loudly, making everyone jump. 'We left him in the shed, remember?'

'Oh, that's right,' Lex's granny said. 'I forgot.'

'Lex went out to get him. Look, there she is!'

On cue, Lex appeared at the kitchen window with the wombat-baby in the woollen blanket, making sure not to stand too close to the glass. Everybody cooed and smiled and I pretended to try and open the back door.

'Oh,' I said, 'it's locked.'

'The key should be in the door,' Lex's mum said.

'It's not.'

'Oh, then it should be on the hook.'

'Nope, not there either.'

'Oh, that's very odd. Wait, how did Lex–?'

'Well, we'd better be going,' I said. 'Dad's doing lasagne tonight, isn't he, Mum?'

'Mmm,' my mum said, 'your favourite. You're right, we must be off; he'll be very put out if it ends up going cold. Lovely to see you all. Bye, Mrs Brooks.'

'Bye bye now, dearie,' Lex's granny said.

I dropped the back-door key into her open hand as I passed. On the walk home I felt very proud of myself. Sometimes I'm almost *too* clever.

As we sat down at the table and Dad dished out the lasagne, I suddenly had a worrying thought.

I hope Lex's mum doesn't plan on using the washing machine this evening.

Chapter Five

I quite like my teacher, Mr Freebs; he never shouts, he gives gold stars for being able to climb the monkey bars or run a full lap of the yard as well as for normal school stuff, and on Friday afternoons he lets us watch 'educational' cartoons (the cartoons aren't always very educational, sometimes they're just fun, but we do have to answer questions at the end of them). Mr Freebs does have one terrible, unforgivable flaw though. He wants everyone to *get along*. And if he thinks you're not *getting along* with someone else in the classroom, he does awful things like making you work with them on a special project, or making you write down five things you like about them.

Mr Freebs has noticed that I don't *get along* with Nathan Wall. This is because Nathan Wall is evil. And he's a snob. He's an evil snob who doesn't have one single likeable quality. Mr Freebs forced me to write down five things I like about Nathan Wall. Here is the list:

1. He lives far away from me.

2. He eats his lunch at a table far away from me.

3. He is not related to me so I'm not forced to see him during holidays.

4. Yesterday his orange juice burst in his schoolbag and he got so mad he nearly cried, which was funny.

5. His mum has some fancy job as a diplomat or something, which means the Walls could be transferred to some faraway place like Timbuktu at any moment.

I looked up the spelling and location of Timbuktu in an atlas, but Mr Freebs still didn't like my list, and on Monday morning I was made to sit next to Nathan at a desk in the front row of the class.

'You know, when people don't like each other,' Mr Freebs said, 'it's often because they don't really know each other. One term of sitting together and I think you two are going to get along just fine.'

The whole TERM?

Mr Freebs had gone too far.

Nathan sat down next to me, took his

stuff out of his bag and immediately put his pencil case on *my* side of the desk. I pushed it back to his side and he said, 'Eh, I need more room for my stuff 'cos it's more valuable. This pencil case is a *Star Wars* original signed by George Lucas. My mum got it at Skywalker Ranch.' He put it back in the middle of the desk. 'Don't put your pencil case near it 'cos it might scrape it. It doesn't matter if yours gets scraped, it's just a cheapo one.'

He grinned at me, sitting there with his greasy hair that had way too much hair gel.

That's another thing I like about Nathan Wall. His hair always looks stupid.

I did a bad thing. A *very* bad thing.

I let slip about the clubhouse.

I didn't mean to, it was an accident. *And* it was a direct result of Nathan Wall being the most annoying and obnoxious human being that's ever lived.

For the whole morning I didn't scream or yell or hit him on the head with my pencil case or anything, for which I think I deserve a medal. But after little break, when we came in from the yard and I had to sit next to him again, I realised the torture was only beginning. I was going to be stuck next to him for *months*. It might as well have been forever.

'And after Disney World we're going to Mexico. We'll be there for three whole weeks and we're staying in a five-star hotel.' Nathan had been going on about his holiday for ages, and it wasn't til June *next year*. 'Have you ever stayed in a five-star hotel? They're the best. It's like everybody who works there is your servant. Where are you going for your summer holidays?'

'I don't know,' I said, trying to concentrate on the picture I was drawing. 'It's only September. The summer holidays are ages away.'

'You have to book five-star hotels in advance,' he said, 'that's why ours is booked already. And Disney World too. We booked really early to make sure we got the best rooms. We're pretty much staying in a castle.'

'Really.' I was leaning so hard on the pencil that it was starting to scrape through the paper.

'Yeah, it'll be awesome. Where are you going on your holidays? Oh, you said, you don't know. It'll probably be that cottage in the west, won't it? You write about that every year when we have to do the "What I did on my holidays" essay. Why do you always go to the same place? You should go somewhere different. You should go abroad. Five-star hotels abroad are the best.'

I finally snapped.

'For your information,' I said, 'I might not even go to the cottage next summer 'cos I've got the coolest place in the world *right here*. I've got a secret clubhouse with my secret gang and we're going to spend the *whole* summer planning cool things and having midnight feasts and making lists of all the things we *don't like* about Nathan Wall.'

It was nearly worth it – *nearly* – to see the look on Nathan's face. For a second he was jealous. Then he grinned his stupid grin and pretended he wasn't.

'Who's in your secret gang?'

'None of your business. It's a secret.'

'Is it Lex?'

'No.'

'And Nicholas?'

'It's not Lex or Nicholas.' I said, 'It's nobody you know. That's why it's called a *secret* gang.'

He was still grinning.

'It *is* Lex and Nicholas. Who else would it be? You're always hanging around with them. Where's your clubhouse?'

My face was feeling kind of prickly and hot, and I was already imagining how I was going to tell the others that I had spilled our secret.

'I'm not telling you where it is 'cos you're not allowed in. We'd never let someone like *you* in our clubhouse.'

'I bet it's rubbish,' Nathan said.

'It's not, it's brilliant. It's the best clubhouse anybody's ever had.'

'I bet it's not, I bet it's rubbish. Where is it?'

I kept my mouth shut from then on, determined not to give any more away, but it was very hard work. I kind of wanted Nathan to see our clubhouse because it really is the best clubhouse anybody's ever had. But the others would kill me if I gave away the secret location.

'How are things at the New Friends' Table?' Mr Freebs came over and smiled at the two of us. 'Getting along?'

Chapter Six

It was Tuesday after school and I was sitting in the Naughty Corner in the clubhouse. That's an actual thing now. It was Lex's idea.

'Like a timeout when you were little,' she said, 'and it's easy, you just have to sit there.'

'I am not sitting in the *Naughty Corner*. I'm ten and a quarter years old,' I said.

'And a hat,' said Nicholas.

'What?'

'You should have to wear a hat while you sit in the Naughty Corner. Something embarrassing to show that you've done something stupid. I've got that jester one I made for the Renaissance Fair.'

'I am *not* sitting in the Naughty Corner and I am *not* wearing a jester's hat!'

This timeout thing was a teeny, tiny bit my own fault. I broke Rule No. 2 of the clubhouse:

2. Never tell anyone outside the Bubble Street Gang about the clubhouse.

And when I wrote the Rules of the Clubhouse I also added the following line at the bottom:

Anyone who breaks any of the

Rules of the

Clubhouse

MUST BE PUNISHED.

Just like that, underlined in big bold letters.

I wasn't specific about what the punishment should be though (I wasn't expecting to be punished myself), which meant Lex and Nicholas had to come up with something they thought was fair. Lex was trying to be nice, making it so I just had to sit in the corner for a while, but I would much rather have handed over a year's pocket money than sit in a timeout like a two-year-old.

So there I was, on a stool in the Naughty Corner in a jester's hat, while Lex and Nicholas had the club meeting without me.

'Can I at least have a cookie?' I said.

'No talking in the Naughty Corner,' Nicholas replied.

I sighed and waited it out.

When the time was up I went straight to the muffin bucket to reward myself for being so good. Thankfully, Lex had saved all the treats from being pulverised in the washing machine.

'I couldn't sleep,' she said, 'thinking Mum or Dad might put on a load of washing in the morning. So I snuck down in the middle of the night.'

She'd stashed the muffins, crisps and other stuff in a pillowcase and hidden them inside the piano in the front room until she could take them out to the clubhouse. I'm glad she did. Secret meetings are so much better with snacks.

'Where did all the mini-muffins go?' I said, disappointed.

'I had one,' Lex replied.

'I had two,' said Nicholas.

'There was a whole packet here,' I said. 'Where are the rest of them?'

The other two shrugged their shoulders and I frowned at them as I took a cookie instead. Somebody was guzzling mini-muffins and fibbing about it.

The missing mini-muffin thing took a serious turn that Saturday. We were all set to spend an entire afternoon in the clubhouse, but when we arrived we noticed something very odd. The door was slightly open.

'Who was last out on Thursday?' I asked.

'Me,' said Nicholas.

'You left the door open.'

'No, I didn't.'

'You did. It's open, look. That's Rule No. 7 you broke.'

'I did *not* forget to close the door.'

I didn't believe him until we went inside and saw crumbs on the table. Rule No. 9 of the clubhouse:

9. If you're eating something crumbly you must use a plate. No one wants mice in the clubhouse.

The table had been squeaky clean when we left it on Thursday evening. I remembered checking.

There could only be one explanation. We had intruders in the clubhouse.

'It's Nathan Wall,' said Nicholas.

'We don't know that for sure,' I said.

'Who else could it be? Who else knows about the clubhouse?'

'Someone could have found it by accident.'

I said the last bit quietly because I didn't think it was possible. I didn't want to be the reason we had intruders in the clubhouse.

'But Nathan Wall doesn't live anywhere near here,' said Lex.

That was true. Nathan lives in a big house at the other end of town. But Sasha Noonan

lives in Berbel Street, and Sasha Noonan is Nathan's best friend. They get along so well because Sasha is also evil. Their other best friend, Jim Brick, lives just one street away.

'They all went to Sasha's house,' Nicholas started.

'And searched until they found the clubhouse,' I finished.

'Or they followed us. Either way, it's theirs now too.'

No way. No *way*.

I couldn't bear it. Nathan Wall and those other snots invading *our* clubhouse, sitting at *our* table, eating *our* mini-muffins. The *humanity*!

'I know you broke into our clubhouse,' I whispered.

It was Monday morning in school and Mr Freebs was drawing the life cycle of the frog on the board. We were supposed to be copying it down, but I was too angry to draw. Nathan gave me a funny look.

'What are you talking about?'

'I know you were in there,' I said, 'you and your snotty friends. But just so you know, we've booby-trapped the place now. Next time you go in you'll set off a tripwire and you'll probably have your head chopped off or end up hanging from your ankles. Just so you know.'

'I didn't break into your stupid clubhouse, why would I? It sounds rubbish.'

'The tripwires are everywhere,' I said, 'so beware.'

We did try setting booby-traps, but it's a lot

more complicated than it looks on TV. The tripwires didn't work and all that happened was Lex got her feet tangled in twine then fell over and banged her head on the table.

By lunchtime no one had confessed, but we weren't giving up that easily. Mr Freebs took us all to the stream near the school to collect slimy things in jars. Nicholas and Sasha got into an argument which ended with her pushing him into the water. He was covered in muck and slimy things and, to add insult to injury, Sasha and Nicholas had to write five things they liked about each other.

Nicholas was furious.

'We can't let those snots get away with it,' he said.

'First things first,' I said, 'we need to catch them in the act.'

And so began the Bubble Street Gang's first mission:

Operation Snot Surveillance.

Chapter Seven

I was still really annoyed that there were intruders in our clubhouse but, I had to admit, I was also a bit excited that the Bubble Street Gang would have to solve a mystery. That was the point of starting the gang in the first place – to investigate mystery, solve crime, start small businesses and generally do exciting stuff.

I'm the brains of the operation. My skills are perfect for solving mysteries and crimes. I'm like a detective: I *observe* things (which means I see things) and then I *deduce* things (which means I work things out). For examples, I *observed* Carol Fletcher picking her nose at the back of class, then I *deduced* that Carol Fletcher is gross.

My brain is a finely-tuned instrument and not everyone can do what I do. It requires patience and attention to detail. Like this one time when I worked out that our neighbour, Mr Arnott, was probably a serial killer because he was always digging in his tomato patch at night. So I waited and waited, and when he went out for the day I dug up the tomato patch looking for bones. But it turned out it was just a tomato patch, and Mr Arnott doesn't give us free vegetables any more.

For Operation Snot Surveillance, Lex, Nicholas and me had to look for clues; *proof* that the snots were using our clubhouse.

On the way back from the yard at the end

of little break, I caught Lex by the arm. 'I need you to distract Nathan so I can search his schoolbag.'

'What?' she said, looking panicked. 'Why me? I can't, don't make me. What would I say?'

I would have asked Nicholas – Lex is not good at chatting to people for no reason – but he'd been called to Ms Bulger's room to prepare for his grass role in the school play.

'You'll be grand,' I said. 'Just improvise, like your granny says. Talk to him, ask him stuff. He loves talking about himself. Just ask him about himself.'

As I hurried to get back to the classroom before anyone else, I heard Lex say behind me, 'Hi, Nathan, how are you?'

'What do you want?'

'Oh, nothing, nothing really. Do you like horse-riding? I heard you do horse-riding. Would you like to be a horse? If you could be any animal in the world, what animal would you be?'

Note to self: When distracting small talk is needed for a mission, pick someone other than Lex.

The classroom was empty. I felt a bit bold – going through someone else's bag could get me in big trouble – but this was official detective business and it had to be done. I went straight for Nathan's schoolbag and tipped it out. There was a shiny keychain with his name on it (but no keys), a Velcro wallet with *forty euros* inside (what ten-year-old has forty euros just sitting in their schoolbag?), a bag of crisps, sandwiches in a fancy *Star Wars* lunchbox (probably a limited edition

signed by Chewbacca) and a scrap of paper. I unrolled the paper and gasped. It was a piece of a map drawn in blue biro. One street was marked *Berbe–*, but the rest had been torn off. *Berbel Street*. It was a map to our clubhouse. It had to be. But why rip it up?

Then it came to me. It was just like a pirate story I'd read during the summer (FYI, all good detectives read lots of books. You wouldn't believe how many brilliant ideas I get from books). Three pirates buried a load of treasure on an island in the middle of the Pacific Ocean, but they didn't really trust each other. So they drew one map to the treasure and tore it into three pieces. That way, years later, they could only find the treasure again by putting all three bits of the map together. It didn't work out that way in the end; one pirate killed another one and took his bit of the map, then the third one disappeared at sea and the treasure was eventually found by an orphan who'd been shipwrecked and landed on the island by mistake.

But anyway, it was clear the snots didn't trust each other (because they're not the best of friends like me and Lex and Nicholas), so they'd each taken a piece of the map to the clubhouse. Now all we needed were the other two pieces from Jim and Sasha and ... *proof!*

There were voices outside the room so I jammed everything back into Nathan's bag (except for the piece of map, which I pocketed) then sat at the desk with my hands clasped like a perfect angel.

'What are you smiling about?' Nathan said as he sat beside me.

'Nothing.'

Note to self: No smiling when you've secretly outwitted your opponent – he might realise you've outwitted him.

Sasha's piece of the map was next on the list. And I knew how we could get hold of that one.

Sasha was playing Maria in *The Sound of Music* – that's the part Julie Andrews played in the film, the part with all the singing. God knows why Ms Bulger gave her that role.

When Sasha sings she sounds like my auntie's cat did right before he died. And having her prance about the stage in a nun's outfit is pure irony.

Definition of irony: someone dancing around in a nun's costume when they are

nothing *like a nun.*

It was the opening night of the school play. Nicholas had been in the worst mood anyone's ever been in, all day. He kept saying it was *demeaning* (I planned to look that up when I got home, but I could guess what it meant) to be playing grass, but I could tell he was also forced to take the part seriously. Because Nicholas always takes acting seriously.

'I absolutely can't,' he said when I told him my plan. 'I'd have to break character.'

'It's *grass.*'

'You're the one who got me into this, now you're saying I have to do a bad job?'

It went on like that for a while until he finally agreed to the plan.

The curtain went back and there was Sasha,

squawking in a wimple.

And there was Nicholas, lying on his front on the stage wrapped in green foam with just a narrow slit for his eyes so he could see out. There was green foam all around him too, so he looked like a little hill in a field. That was the worst I ever felt about the whole thing. Sasha stepped on him twice.

The plan was carried out backstage during an indoor scene when the grass wasn't needed. Sasha has a little square backpack with a dolphin on it that she never takes off, even in class. That's why it had to be done during the play. I told Nicholas to wave to me during the next mountain scene if he managed to get the map piece from Sasha's backpack. He flat-out refused.

'Break the fourth wall and interact with

the audience?' he said. 'Are you nuts?'

So I had to wait until the play was over. While my parents told Nicholas's dad what good grass Nicholas had been, and Nicholas's dad went on about how it was a waste of talent, Nicholas handed me a curled bit of torn paper. It fit perfectly with the piece from Nathan's schoolbag. There was *Berbel Street* and next to it, torn on the last word, *McCall's Fie–*

'We've got them now,' said Nicholas.

'Not quite,' I said. 'This doesn't have the hedge and the clubhouse. We need the last piece.'

Watch out Jim Brick, the Bubble Street Gang is coming for you.

Chapter Eight

'It's not in his bag.'

'What?'

'It's not in his schoolbag.'

Nicholas was paired with Jim for the 'Making a Rocket' art project, and he took the chance to search Jim's bag.

'It must be in there,' I said. 'Where else could it be?'

'Maybe he left it at home,' said Lex.

I thought this through. It was possible, but improbable. Jim has a million brothers and sisters. It's not actually a million – I think there's seven kids in the family – but I do know he shares a room with his little brother

Brian (who is not as small as the annoying baby twins, but is nearly as annoying) and he also has an older sister, Lisa, who is about the nosiest parker you could ever meet. I'd say keeping secrets in the Brick household is a challenge and, if I were Jim, I'd keep a secret piece of a secret map somewhere else.

'The football club!' I said suddenly.

'Do you think?' said Lex.

'Definitely. He's there every other day.'

Jim's on the local team and they take training very seriously. The club is next to the football pitch. I've never seen it up close, but I'd say it's easy enough to break into.

'Isn't that a crime?' Lex said, worried.

'No,' I said. 'Well maybe, a bit, I'm not sure. But we won't get caught. And even if we do we can explain it all to the police and

I'm sure they'd understand.'

Lex went white.

'We're not breaking into the football club,' Nicholas said. 'Besides, they might have their own lockers in there with combination locks. We wouldn't be able to get one of those open.'

'Then that's where his bit of the map would be!' I said. 'Where better to hide it than a locker with an unbreakable lock?'

'We are not breaking into the football club.'

I sighed.

'How about this? I'll find out whether or not they've got lockers with combination locks at the football club, and if they *don't* we won't bother breaking in. He wouldn't hide the map where it wouldn't be safe.'

'And if they *do* have lockers with combination locks?' said Nicholas.

'Well then,' I said, avoiding his gaze, 'we'll have some serious thinking to do.'

Carl is on the local football team as well. He gave me weird looks when he noticed me following him around school.

'What do you want?' he asked.

'Oh, I was just wondering about starting football over at the Redz club.'

He looked at me even weirder – I'm not into any sports at school, I complain when we have to play table tennis.

'Not for me,' I said quickly, 'for Lex. She's too shy to ask.'

That made more sense. Lex is good at every sport she tries.

'What does she want to know?' said Carl.

'Do you get your own locker?'

'That's what she wants to know about playing football for the Redz?'

'Yep. Safe place to keep her stuff, she's all about that. Something with a combination lock would be good.'

'There are lockers, but no combination locks. You just use whichever one is free during practice.'

'Cheers, Carl. Thanks for the info.'

He called out to me as I walked away. 'Does she want me to sign her up?'

'No thanks. The combination lock was a deal-breaker.'

Lex and I were crouched down behind a car. We were spying – actual *spying* – on Jim Brick. We'd followed him all the way from school, ducking behind walls and peeking from behind the trees. I was born for this. At one point I did a tuck-and-roll from a lamp-post to a postbox. I didn't really have to, but it looked cool.

Jim went into the football club, but luckily it was just to pick something up from his coach; it would have been really boring if we'd had to wait for a whole football practice, especially since we'd no need to sneak in like cat burglars now. After the club, Jim went into a sweet shop, then he headed home.

He was walking the narrow parkway between Mole Road and Lawson Street – it's a few rows of trees and an old stone wall – when he ducked down behind the wall.

'Oh no,' I said from behind a tree trunk, 'we can't get closer without him seeing us.'

'Hold on,' Lex said, and then she was off.

Like the tailless monkey she is, she was up the first tree and swinging to the next before I knew it. A few moments later she was hanging upside down from the knees right above the wall. As long as Jim didn't look up – and why would he? – he'd never see her.

It felt like forever, but finally Lex swung back to me and scurried down a tree trunk.

'He's gone,' she said, 'but there's a hole in the wall. He hid something in there.'

Lex showed me the spot, but it still took a few minutes to find the right stone. One of them was loose and it came out with some wiggling.

'Wow,' I said when I saw the safe little space inside, 'Jim must be the smartest of the snots.'

Inside was a packet of jellies, three lolli-pops, a butterfly hair clip that I recognised as Sally Benson's – he must fancy her, that's hilarious – and a rolled-up bit of paper.

There it was, the last piece of the map. I put the three pieces together and frowned. Lex frowned too.

'That's not where the clubhouse is,' she said.

There was a big red X near the bottom of the map, but whatever it was it wasn't our clubhouse.

All three of us – Lex, Nicholas and me – were following the snots' map, walking down the lane next to Berbel Street. We passed Mr McCall's field but didn't go in (*unrelated fact: the bull is gone, so no snorting security any-*

more. Oh, well). We kept walking until we got to the field beyond. It's not a completely empty one. They were going to build houses there, but stopped once they got a few of the foundations in, so now it's a weird kind of graveyard for houses that never were.

'Ten paces from the redbrick square,' Nicholas said, reading the map.

There is only one house-grave where the foundations are topped with a layer of red brick.

'Ten paces?' I said as we counted ten paces. 'Do they think they're pirates? What's a pace anyway?'

'A step,' said Nicholas.

'Yeah, but everybody's got a different size step, so is it ten of *my* steps, ten of *your* steps, ten of Lex's–'

'Five paces east,' Nicholas interrupted.

'East? What am I, a sailor? Where's east?'

'Back towards Berbel Street.'

'Then why don't they just say that?'

'There's something here!' Lex said.

Her foot had banged off something half buried in the gravelly ground. We scraped and dug and eventually pulled up a metal box about the size of a small lunchbox.

'It's not locked or anything,' I said, rolling my eyes. 'Amateurs.'

We opened it up and inside was a weird collection of objects. There was a shiny key-ring (a different colour to the one in Nathan's bag, but still with his name on it), a really old postcard with a picture of a dolphin under-water (on the other side there was scribbly writing, 'My dearest Sasha …' We couldn't read the rest but it ended with, 'Love always, Grandad') and a football medal from the year before. There were other little things too – a pack of cards, a travel game of Ludo and a packet of jelly beans. Underneath it all was a carefully folded piece of paper. I opened it and read, 'Rules for the Na-Sa-Ji Club. Rule One, never speak the name of the club to anyone outside the club. Rule Two, each club meeting must begin with the secret club handshake. Rule Three ...'

There were about twenty rules. I didn't read them all out.

'Whoa,' said Lex, 'they've got their own club. What does Na-Sa-Ji mean?'

'It's the first two letters of all of their names,' I said.

'Oh, that's clever.'

'I don't know, sounds kind of lame to me.'

Lex picked up the dolphin postcard.

'I think Sasha's grandad died last year. Remember? She was out for a couple of days.'

'They all must have put one thing that's really important to them in the box,' said Nicholas.

We all went quiet for a minute. It was weird. It was like we were a bit embarrassed to have found something so private, like we'd just walked in on somebody in the bathroom or something.

It made me feel a bit sad, but also a bit happy. They've only got a club-*box*, we've got a club-*house*. I imagined bragging to Nathan back at school, but then I felt I didn't really need to. I was in the best club ever. And I knew it.

'I think we should put it back,' I said.

'Me too,' said Lex.

'We can put back the map pieces as well,' said Nicholas, 'so they never need to know we found it.'

We all agreed and reburied the box.

The next day, at school, Nathan put his pencil case in the middle of our desk again. I didn't get mad. He made fun of my drawing in art. I didn't get mad. He told me that his mum got VIP tickets for some concert and that my mum couldn't get VIP tickets for anything because we weren't rich. I still didn't get mad.

I don't know why, but none of it made me angry that day. I just felt all glowy and wholesome and smiled at him whenever he was rude. In the end, my not getting angry made him furious. It was a lovely day. Only one worrying thought stopped it from being a perfect day.

If the snots aren't using our clubhouse, who is?

Chapter Nine

```
┌─────────────────────────────────────────────────┐
│                                                 │
│                  EXHIBIT A                      │
│  ─────────────────────────────────────────────  │
│                                                 │
│  Animal hair; short, orangey-white, and there's loads of it │
│                                                 │
└─────────────────────────────────────────────────┘
```

The clubhouse was still being invaded. The next Saturday afternoon we arrived to find three of Nicholas's dad's flapjacks missing (there were just a few oaty crumbs left) and some orangey-white hair on the ground. I picked it up and examined it with a magnifying glass.

'Almost certainly animal,' I said.

I'm a detective, I know these things.

'What kind of animal?' asked Lex.

'Almost certainly cat, or almost certainly dog.'

I wasn't sure, but I figured I couldn't go wrong with cat or dog.

'It could be a ferret,' said Nicholas.

'It's not a ferret.'

'Ferrets are wild, aren't they? There could be some living around here.'

'Impossible,' I said, 'there are no ferrets in this part of the country.'

I didn't really know what a ferret was.

'So there's a cat or a dog sneaking in and stealing our snacks?' said Lex.

'Mmm,' I said, narrowing my eyes. 'And I think I know exactly which cat or dog it is.'

Mr Dixon's cat is very fat. At least I think it is. It's a huge big ball of orange and white fur, and it's hard to tell how much of the fur is cat and how much of the fur is just fur.

The cat's name is Bless (I know, ridiculous name for a cat) and Lex told me it was a *him* so I'll call it a him from now on.

You can probably tell that I don't like Mr Dixon's cat very much. Bless (ugh, I can't get past that terrible name) is the laziest, most *confrontational* cat ever. It was my mum who called him confrontational. She called him that because he has this habit of sitting in the middle of the path, right where you're headed, and refusing to move. He just sits there with his lazy eyes half-closed as if he's saying, 'Just go around me, human. I'm far too important to move out of your way.'

But you don't want to go around him because he's just a cat and he should move instead of sitting in the middle of the path in your way. So you stay on course. You walk closer and closer, refusing to go around him. And he just sits there and sits there and refuses to move. It's like a really slow game of chicken. Which you always lose.

Bless never moves. He watches you out of the corner of his half-closed eyes as you walk around him, and I'd swear he's smiling when he does it.

Well, on the Saturday the Bubble Street Gang came looking for him, Bless's number was up. I was sure it was him who was scoffing our muffins and flapjacks (it's easy to believe he's greedy as well as lazy) and I was going to prove it by getting a sample of his fur.

We went back to Berbel Street, and there he was, sitting in the middle of the path outside Mr Dixon's house. So predictable.

'When we get close enough,' I said, 'you guys grab him so I can pluck a few hairs.'

'He'll run away before we get close enough,' Nicholas said. He'd started tiptoeing.

'No, he won't. He'll sit right there, right in the middle of the path, expecting us to go around him. Well, not today. Today, Mr Bless, your bad manners are going to be your downfall.'

'What if he scratches?' Lex said. She was tiptoeing too, and her hands were shaking a little.

'He won't scratch.'

'What if he bites?'

'He won't bite.'

'What if—?'

'Just grab him, Lex, and I'll do the rest.'

We got a bit closer. The half-closed eyes

watched as if the cat was bored. We got closer again and the tail twitched, but the cat didn't move. We inched closer and closer and I'd swear the cat was smirking. We were nearly there, just a few more steps, Nicholas and Lex reached out their hands, gently grabbed the giant ball of fur and – '*YEOWWWW*!'

It was like an orange and white tornado suddenly sprang from the ground. There were claws and teeth and horrible screeching sounds, and then the orange and white thing darted down the wall to the side of Mr Dixon's house and vanished out the back.

'Huh,' I said, catching my breath, 'that didn't go very well.'

Lex and Nicholas stared at me – they both had scratches all over their hands and arms, I had none. I tried to be upbeat about it.

'Plan B,' I said. 'And don't worry, this one will be far less dangerous.'

I have this claw thing that my uncle gave me for my birthday. It's about half a metre long with a handle at one end and a two-fingered claw at the other. You squeeze the handle and you can pick up stuff with the claw; something that might be too high to reach, for example, or something that's unexpectedly vicious and you'd prefer not to get too close to. With the claw, my friends and I could now safely collect a sample of Bless's fur from a distance ... a bit of a distance anyway.

We sat on the wall at the end of Mr Dixon's back garden. Bless sat in the middle of the grass, twitching his tail, laughing at us (probably). There was a large willow tree on one side of the garden, with branches that drooped nearly all the way to the grass.

'Lex,' I said, acting casual, 'could I get onto that tree from the wall?'

'Yeah, sure,' she replied. 'Just walk this wall, turn onto the side wall, and hop onto one of the branches.'

'Which branch?'

'Em, that one there, look. That would do.'

'Wouldn't I fall off the branch?'

'No, no, just remember to keep your balance. And you can always hold on to the one above it if you start to wobble.'

'Hmm, I'm wearing kind of slippery shoes. What if my feet slip?'

'Oh, then I guess just keep a hold of the top branch so you don't fall off.'

'And what if–?'

Nicholas interrupted by sighing loudly. 'She wants *you* to hop onto the tree and get the fur sample, Lex.'

I was hoping Lex would offer to do it if I kept on asking questions. Nicholas ruined it. I scowled at him.

'Really?' said Lex.

'Well,' I said, 'I don't *mind* doing it, but I'm much more likely to fall. I mean, I don't *mind*.'

Lex gave a sad sigh like she was about to walk the plank. 'All right, I'll do it. Give me the claw.'

'Thanks, Lex.'

The walk down the wall went fine, and the hop to the tree went fine, and the dangling from the tree upside down while holding the claw went fine. It was all going fine, and as

Lex reached down with the claw even the cat looked fine about it. Then there was a sudden bang and lots of screaming.

I should have mentioned earlier that Mr Dixon is about as likeable as his cat. He doesn't like anyone going near his garden, and he especially doesn't like anyone sneaking *into* his garden. He sprang from the back door swinging a golf club like a golf-club-wielding maniac, screaming his head off.

'Brutes!' he yelled. 'Get off my wall, get out of my tree, leave my cat alone!'

He had a point about all of the above, but he could have just *asked*. Screaming and swinging a golf club made us all immediately terrified. Nicholas fell off the wall, Lex fell out of the tree and sprinted down the grass, and it was only because I am so cool in a crisis that I was able to keep my balance long enough to grab Lex's hand and pull her out of the garden.

We ran down the green behind the houses until we couldn't hear Mr Dixon screaming anymore.

'I think my heart nearly stopped!' Nicholas said, wheezing. 'That was scary.'

'And pointless,' I said. 'We didn't get a sample of that horrible cat's fur.'

'Oh, didn't we?'

Lex was grinning, holding up the claw. There, pinched between the two plastic fingers were a few strands of orange and white hair.

'Lex,' I said, 'you're a legend.'

'I know.'

Chapter Ten

Bless was innocent. Of breaking into our clubhouse anyway. Of being a horrible, lazy, chicken-playing cat he was definitely *not* innocent. But he wasn't the intruder.

I examined the two hair samples under a microscope (that's right, I've got a microscope, just like Sherlock Holmes. If you don't know who Sherlock Holmes is, check him out. He's awesome). The two samples didn't match. The hairs from the clubhouse were shorter and, under the microscope, they looked more tan-coloured than orangey-white.

'I think,' I said with my best scientist face,

'that these hairs are actually canine in origin.'

'What does that mean?' said Lex.

'It means they're from a dog. And it means I know who the intruder is. And as it's nearly five o'clock I know exactly where she'll be.'

Bianca is a few years older than us. She's in big school (that is, secondary school), so she thinks she's the bee's knees. I don't think Bianca is the bee's knees, I think she's the wasp's bottom.

Part of what makes Bianca think she's so cool is that she has a job. She's a dog-walker. Every day, at around five o'clock, she takes a whole bunch of dogs from the street to the park. There's a big red setter, a medium-sized poodle, one collie, two Jack Russells and a couple of Chihuahuas. It was the Chihuahuas I was interested in. They're those little dogs that look like large rats with huge, bulgy eyes. They're also tan-coloured, like the hairs from the clubhouse.

While following Bianca and the dogs to the park I had to give Nicholas loads of instructions. He'd missed out on following Jim Brick so he didn't have the spying experience that me and Lex had.

'Duck down,' I'd say. 'Keep your feet in. Don't talk. Keep your eyes on the target at all times. No, not like that, like this. Get behind this tree!'

'Stop telling me what to do,' he said.

If he'd just done what I told him to, I wouldn't have had to tell him what to do.

Bianca stood in the park in a pair of over-sized sunglasses, holding her mobile phone

to her ear with one hand and all the dog leads in the other.

'She kind of looks like a movie star,' whispered Lex as we hunkered down behind a pillar.

'She looks like an idiot,' I said. 'Unless you think movie stars look like idiots, then she looks like a movie star *and* an idiot.'

'There's no way she brought all those dogs to our clubhouse,' Nicholas said.

'No,' I replied, 'but people who live and work with dogs get dog hairs on their clothes. Then they *leave* dog hairs wherever they go. I'm telling you, she's the intruder.'

'But how are we going to prove it?'

'I need a hair sample from her jumper.'

'Great. How are we going to get that?'

'You and Lex are going to distract her while

I sneak up from behind and snag a few hairs.'

Lex looked worried. 'I'm not good at distracting people with talking.'

'No, you're not,' I agreed. 'That's why Nicholas is going with you. He could talk someone to sleep.'

'You're hilarious,' Nicholas groaned.

'I know. Now go and distract her.'

I stayed hunkered down behind the pillar while the other two approached Bianca.

'Hey, Bianca,' said Nicholas, 'cool sunglasses. They kind of make you look like a movie star.'

Bianca looked at him like he was an eejit. 'Eh, that's the idea.'

''Course it is. Have you ever thought about acting? I bet you could make it in the movies. I do a bit of acting myself.'

'Yeah, my little sister was in *The Sound of Music*. I saw you playing grass.'

Touché, Bianca. Turns out the wasp's bottom's got a nasty sting. Poor Nicholas.

While he tried to make his first acting role sound slightly less embarrassing, I crept up behind Bianca like a ninja. I was so close now I could see the dog hairs on her jumper. There was a selection; longish red ones, black and white ones, and there, in the middle of her back, tan-coloured ones. The mission was on.

The dogs were also distracted by Lex and Nicholas; they jumped up on them and barked and wagged their tails. Nobody could see me coming. I was right behind Bianca and, in my eagerness not to miss grabbing a hair, I leaned in too far and pinched too hard.

'*Owwww!*'

Bianca howled like a banshee at a yodelling contest. The dogs went nuts.

It was carnage. My sudden appearance had startled some of the smaller dogs and they yipped and pranced around like the park was on fire. That and Bianca's scream scared the bigger dogs and they started running around in circles. Pretty soon Bianca was wrapped in dog leads, like a leash mummy. She fell over, still yelling, and the dogs jumped all over her. They were wagging their tails and barking happily now – they thought it was a game.

'Cass Okara, I'm going to tell your *mum*!' Bianca screeched.

It was time for us to leave. When we ran out the entrance of the park Bianca was still lying in the grass, covered in dogs.

Bianca was innocent. Bianca is also alive and well, I saw her in the street a few days later (I hid behind a wall). She didn't tell my mum about the incident in the park – I can only guess she was too embarrassed to explain how she lost control of the dogs. Her job is more important to her than revenge.

The hairs from Bianca's jumper didn't match those from the clubhouse.

'What now?' said Lex.

'There's only one thing left to do,' I said.

'What?'

'We'll have to stake out our own club-house.'

And that's exactly what we did. Two Saturday afternoons in a row there had been evidence of the intruders, so we figured Saturday morning was the best time to catch them.

We headed out early – ten o'clock – to get there before them, and we figured no one in their right mind would be up and about before ten o'clock on a Saturday morning. We were wrong. As we approached the hedge from the stream side we could hear voices.

'They're already in there!' cried Lex.

'Perfect,' I said, 'then we've caught them red-handed.'

We crept to the edge of the stream, but didn't cross the plank-bridge. There were a lot of voices.

'How many of them are there?' whispered Nicholas.

'I don't know,' I said, 'and I don't care.

They're in our clubhouse, and they're going to have to leave *or else*.'

'Or else what?'

'Just *or else*,' I said testily.

There really were a lot of voices. The clubhouse must have been full.

'Who wants to lead the charge?' I said, hoping to inspire someone else to cross the bridge first.

There was silence. It was going to have to be me. But before I could set foot on the bridge, Nicholas suddenly yelled, 'Come out of that clubhouse, in the name of the law!'

The door burst open and people came flooding out. We couldn't get a good look at them through the hedge, but they were escaping through the field on the other side.

'After them!' I yelled, punching the air.

Nicholas and Lex followed me over the bridge. I sprinted through the hedge and leapt into Mr McCall's field. What I saw nearly knocked me off my feet.

Grannies.

There were grannies everywhere.

Not just grannies, grandads too. Eight or nine of them running through the field and hurling themselves over the fences either side.

'What is going *on*?' said Lex.

'I have no idea,' I said.

Back in the clubhouse the table and chairs had been overturned in the scramble to escape. We set about straightening the place out.

While clearing up a spilled deck of cards I

looked down at the long curtain that covered the window. There was a pair of shoes sticking out from under the material.

I put my finger to my lips and pointed it out to Lex and Nicholas. Then, with my heart pounding in my ears, I tiptoed forward and pulled the curtain back.

'Ah. Hello, dearies.'

'Gran!' cried Lex.

Chapter Eleven

'So, we're rumbled,' Lex's granny said, taking a seat at the table. 'Well done. What gave us away? George can be messy with crumbs, I know, and Maureen's a divil for leaving dog hairs everywhere. That Trixie animal of hers sheds like a weeping willow. I swear, I could follow that woman all over town just by the trail of little blonde hairs.'

'Gran,' said Lex, 'what on earth are you doing here?'

'Oh, you know, eating snacks, playing cards – I had a nifty hand of poker there before you lot scattered the others to the wind – just hanging out generally, having some quiet time away from the kids and grandkids. I mean, we love you all but you can be a bit much sometimes.'

None of us had any idea what to say, so we just sat and stared at the old woman. Finally, she smiled.

'I am sorry we invaded your space. And I betrayed your confidence, I know that, but as soon as you kids mentioned building a clubhouse I thought, "Brilliant. Somewhere we can go and hang out and play cards and just be ourselves." Being an adored and adoring grandmother is no walk in the park, you know. That sweet granny act is a full-time job.'

Lex's grandmother was many things, but I'd never really thought of her as a 'sweet granny'.

'What are we going to do now?' Lex asked nobody in particular.

Suddenly I was angry. Okay, Lex's granny *did* suggest the spot for the clubhouse, but this was *our* clubhouse. We built it, we decorated it and we filled it with snacks, which Lex's granny did give us, but still. It was where *we* went to get away from everything and just be ourselves.

'Well, I'm sorry, Mrs Brooks,' I said in my most formal voice possible, 'but we can't allow you and your friends to invade the clubhouse anymore. This is our place. You're barred.'

Lex looked shocked. Her granny looked amused.

'Oh, you won't know we're here,' she said. 'We'll pop in for a quick game when you lot are at school or away on your holidays. We'll be like little mice.'

'I don't like mice, and I won't have them in my clubhouse. If you don't keep out then we'll have to … we'll have to …'

'You'll have to what, dearie?'

'I don't know, but we'll do something. We'll booby-trap the place, or put a lock on the door. If you sneak in through the window, we'll bar the window. If you sneak in through the roof, we'll … we'll pull down the roof! We'll do whatever we have to do to keep you out because this is our place – *ours* – and you're not having it.'

It felt like there was fire behind my eyes as I stared at Lex's granny. She stared right back, for the longest time. Finally something changed in her eyes and she nodded.

'I appreciate a girl who stands up for herself. You're absolutely right. This is your place and I have no right to be here.'

She stood and pulled her cardigan closed, then smiled and headed for the door. Before leaving she gave us a wave.

'Bubble Street Gang,' she said (don't ask me how Lex's granny knew the secret name of our secret club), 'I salute you. Best of luck in all your endeavours.'

She disappeared out the door and the clubhouse seemed very, very quiet. Nicholas didn't say anything, I didn't say anything, and Lex looked ready to cry. After a minute I bolted out the door.

'Mrs Brooks,' I yelled to the figure traipsing across the field, 'wait!'

Lex's granny paused to look back and I ran

towards her. Behind me I could hear Nicholas and Lex running too.

'What if,' I said, trying to catch my breath, 'what if we built you a clubhouse of your own?'

'What's that now, dearie?' she said, surprised.

'A clubhouse of your own – like ours, but not ours – where you could go and play cards and … hang out with your friends.'

Nicholas and Lex had caught up to us by now and they were nodding.

'It wouldn't take long,' Nicholas said. 'We built our one really quickly.'

'We could even steal some snacks for you too,' said Lex. 'You helped us steal the first pillow-case-full anyway.'

'You can have some of my dad's flapjacks. We'll halve them with you,' said Nicholas.

'Well now,' Lex's granny looked more emotional than I thought she could ever look, 'that is very, very kind. But where would you build it?'

I looked back at the hedge.

'There's plenty of room there,' I said. 'We could build it a few trees down from ours. We'd be neighbours.'

'Hmm.' The woman looked down at the hedge and smiled. 'That sounds like a plan.'

So the granny clubhouse was built, about four trees down from our own so we couldn't hear too much of them (they can get a bit rowdy from time to time). We didn't have another paddling pool so they made a roof by sewing lots of old waterproof jackets together (it actually keeps the rain out better than our roof). They've got awful flowery curtains, a tea-set, a camping stove for boiling the kettle, there are doilies under everything (you know, those terrible little mats that look like snow-flakes) and one of them is a big fan of por-celain figures because there are clowns and angels looking down at you from every shelf. It's kind of spooky. And I think all their stuff came from their attics too because the whole place smells really musty.

At first it was a bit weird having them as neighbours. We would walk across Mr McCall's field with Lex's granny each Satur-day. A row of grannies and grandads would be sitting on the fence at the corner of the field. They'd all say 'hello' and pinch our cheeks and call us cute, the way grandpar-ents are supposed to, then we'd go our sep-arate ways – them to their poker games and cups of tea, us to our chocolate chip cookies and planning our wild adventures.

After a while it was a little less weird. I decided since our clubhouse was no longer guarded by a fierce, snorting bull, it was no harm to be neighbours with a diabolical genius and her friends. If the Na-Sa-Ji club ever *did* find the secret location

of our clubhouse, I've no doubt Lex's granny could scare them off better than a raging bull. In the end, the Bubble Street Gang decided, by vote, to put up with our strange neighbours for as long as they wanted to be there.

Time went by and things got kind of quiet for the Bubble Street Gang. We didn't have any mysteries or crimes to solve, and most of our meetings became about whose turn it was to re-stock the snack jars. We were dying for some real adventure.

Then one day we stepped into the clubhouse and there was an envelope lying on the floor. Someone had slipped it under the door.

'What is it?' said Lex as I opened it.

I read it aloud.

To the Bubble Street Gang,

It is a little-known fact that many, many years ago a rich and greedy Lord owned these lands. He gave nothing to the poor or even to his family, and kept his most precious of precious things safely hidden in a small, wooden trunk. He buried the trunk in a secret location, never to be revealed for he died just days after hiding it away. But somebody somewhere did guess the location of that trunk, and they left crafty clues so that only the bravest and brainiest and quickest of gangs might ever recover it.

Your mission, should you choose to accept it, is to find that box as quickly as possible. Solve the following riddle to locate the next clue:

Normally I guzzle lots
Of shirts and jumpers, pants and socks

But now and then I like to eat
A very different kind of treat
Chocolate, crisps and muffins too
Were hidden in my mouth, yoo-hoo!
But now there is no single trace
Of sweets moved to a pillow case

What am I?

We were all quiet until Lex suddenly shouted, 'Washing machine! The answer is my washing machine!'

We were all grinning widely at each other.

'Well,' said Nicholas, 'what now?'

'What now?' I said. 'Now we go to Lex's house, get the next clue and find the Lord's treasure.'

'Are you sure?' said Lex with a grin. 'I

mean, it's just a treasure hunt for fun. Aren't we supposed to be having real adventures?'

'Oh, there'll be real adventures,' I said, 'plenty of them, with danger and excitement and everything. So we better start practicing our detective skills right away. To Lex's house!'

The other two cheered and we giggled as we hurried out the clubhouse door. I was wrong; it isn't all right being neighbours with a diabolical genius.

It's AWESOME.

CLUBHOUSE RULES

1.THE BUBBLE STREET GANG IS A SECRET ORGANISATION — NEVER REVEAL ITS EXISTENCE.

2. NEVER TELL ANYONE OUTSIDE THE BUBBLE STREET GANG ABOUT THE CLUBHOUSE.

3.THE BUBBLE STREET GANG SWEARS TO SEARCH OUT ADVENTURE, SOLVE MYSTERIES, FIGHT FOR JUSTICE AND BE GOOD ~~ENTERPRINEERS~~ ~~ENTREPENORS~~ BUSINESSPEOPLE.

4.NO FRUIT, BROWN BREAD OR OTHER HEALTHY FOOD IS TO BE CONSUMED IN THE CLUBHOUSE.

5.THE CLUBHOUSE LIBRARY IS FOR EXCITING, DANGEROUS, DETECTIVE OR FUNNY BOOKS ONLY. NO SCHOOLBOOKS.

6.MEMBERS WILL TAKE TURNS TO REFILL THE SNACK JARS.

7.ALWAYS CLOSE THE CLUBHOUSE DOOR WHEN YOU ARE LAST OUT.

8.SECRET DOCUMENTS MUST BE LOCKED AWAY IN THE HARRY POTTER BOOK-SAFE DURING THE NIGHT.

9.IF YOU'RE EATING SOMETHING CRUMBLY YOU MUST USE A PLATE. NO-ONE WANTS MICE IN THE CLUBHOUSE.

10.ANY MEMBER CAN DEMAND HELP FROM OTHER MEMBERS IN MATTERS OF LIFE OR DEATH (OR IF IT'S JUST REALLY, REALLY IMPORTANT).

ANYONE WHO BREAKS ANY OF THE RULES OF THE CLUBHOUSE MUST BE PUNISHED.

Coming soon ...

*Cass and the Bubble Street Gang -
Making Millions*

The Bubble Street Gang is in a pickle.

There's a big, important costume-making class in town
and Nicholas just has to go.
But where will he get the money?

Cass decides it's about time
the Bubble Street Gang became ...

Millionaires!